BOOKS BY ED DORN

POETRY

The Newly Fallen: Poems
Hands Up!
From Gloucester Out
Geography
Idaho Out
The North Atlantic Turbine
Twenty-Four Love Songs
Songs: Set Two - A Short Count
Recollections of Gran Apacheria
Collected Poems
Manchester Square (*with Jennifer Dunbar*)
Gunslinger
Hello, La Jolla

PROSE

What I See in the Maximus Poems
The Rites of Passage: A Brief History
    (*revised later as* By the Sound)
Some Business Recently Transacted in the
    White World
Views & Interviews

NONFICTION

The Shoshoneans: The People of the Basin-Plateau
    (*with photographs by Leroy Lucas*)

TRANSLATION (*with Gordon Brotherston*)

The Tree Between Two Walls
Our Word: Guerilla Poems from Latin America
Cesar Vallejo Selected Poems

SCREENPLAY

Abilene! Abilene!

YELLOW LOLA
FORMERLY TITLED JAPANESE NEON
(HELLO LA JOLLA, *BOOK II*)
ED DORN

CADMUS EDITIONS   SANTA BARBARA
1981

Yellow Lola, formerly titled *Japanese Neon*
(Hello, La Jolla Book II)
Copyright © 1980 by Ed Dorn
Dark Mist by David Hockney copyright © 1973, 1980
by Gemini G.E.L.
Portrait of Ed Dorn by Tom Clark copyright © 1980
by Tom Clark

All rights reserved
Printed in the United States of America

Grateful acknowledgement is extended by
the publisher to David Hockney and Sidney
Felsen of Gemini G.E.L. for their kind
permission for use of *Dark Mist* on the
cover of this book.

First published in 1980 by:
Cadmus Editions
Box 4725
Santa Barbara
California 93103

Dorn, Edward, 1929-
LCN 80-68260
ISBN 0-932274-13-7 (trade edition)
ISBN 0-932274-14-5 (signed edition)

Introduction, Epigraph, Dedication and Notes

Introduction

Yellow Lola, formerly titled *Japanese Neon* would probably not have been published, in this way, if Tom Clark had not come to town and fished it out of my notebook while he was hunting presumably bigger game with perhaps less pleasure.

I recognize in this text the Other book, the psychologically primary hue. When I came to fabricate the sections of *Hello, La Jolla,* I chose those writings which spoke artfully or artlessly, cousins of the same mode.

What we see here is the more or less raw thought, of which *Hello, La Jolla* is the product. Only someone with splintered knees could see these dispatches as "out takes."

Edward Dorn
Boulder, 29 Mayo, 1980

The works to be found herein comprise fragments, lines, aphorisms, epigrams and other examples of poetic sub-strata from Ed Dorn's late 1970's Notebooks, selected and in some cases arranged by Tom Clark, who here serves the function of literary geologist. This is not the whole glittering range of statements the Notebooks contain, but it is one bright piece of the rock.

Tom Clark
Boulder, 6 July, 1980

Epigraph

"Let my fleet of trucks prosper."
Alhaja-Anon

Dedication

If one thinks
of it, a lot of people come to mind.
A book which is defined by
work procedures might be
for nearly anyone, and in that
spirit I want to inscribe this book
——— to my friends ———

Note 1: The Address

The address is to La Jolla because it is the
supremest social terminal I've witnessed.
Of course the moraine contains much rock of foreign
lithology.

Note 2: The Procedure

The 101 section was written while driving to the city on 101
with one hand tied to the wheel. Certain illegalities must
be practiced simply not to waste time. The trick is to write
clearly without taking one's eyes off the road. A certain open
scrawl while one's eyes are fixed is the only trick to be
mastered.

Yellow Lola, formerly titled
Japanese Neon

Tuesday 2 March 1976: Weather Report

The sky for sure
is soup de jour

Environmental carcinogens
and large bowel cancer
go together like marble steps
and fancy dancers

18

(101)

cultural ideal imbalanced:
"weight loss without eating less"

a painful devaluation

19

The Rezanov film script

Nowhere more definitively than in the Alaska of the 18th century did the two minor nations, Russia & the United States (one old & subjected, the other not yet born) meet & cross their futures

"The glad bright wine of adventure filled their veins"

20

Alaska wants to be a nation
and not just another state like Texas

21

Loose goose, tight shoes & cold igloos

One mildly electric campaign
the joke of 1976
possessed one point of interest
namely the amount of Euphemism
generated by what were
originally Euphemisms

Political?

You holding that little piece of paper
up to me and saying it's political?

Sure, it's as political as a gopher hole.
If you were political

you'd have to be running for office
or at *least* investigating somebody

and then you wouldn't even use that word
unless you intended to attack

behind a quite carefully laid plan
or *plan*,† as they say in mexican

---

† Sonido parecido al de la *a* español
en *caso, squat, quantity, wash, wander, watch.*

A Discovery

The extremest pleasure
(is) to step on the Devil's neck,
and yet to enjoy the use of him
                          29 September

101

He was sidetracked
by the molecular structure
of Bricks
at 3:60 PM, the merest
shade before four

The Fence, or the Bauhaus Outhouse

It looks dated enough.
But it wouldn't *stop* a discussion
let alone a mongol.

Proposition 13

People who associate themselves
with dogs
are basically dishonest.

Sometime, the scent of fear sweeps over us
deep into the ice, searching for an opening
our frail hull liable to crack
from the pressure all about us

Public Notice

Don't use my name
Unless you love me
But if you do & you don't
Send me some money

Trees

We must remember that the tree
was a living tree   Then it was brought
inside the house where it never wanted to be
(Otherwise) As far as I can guess
Barbara Streisand made Christmas

A Pontificatory use of the art
is both interesting & a lot of fun
the pope's got a really good role

31

the boundary condition

my boy, always remember one thing
If you can't boost, don't knock
                              (from Rex Beach)

group analysis

They were held together
by a more or less passionate
hatred of Barbara Streisand.
A sound basis for a relationship
but not a wide one.

What's that for?   (Throw-weight)

I'm making a dogshit catapult
which I hope to market to people
who live on precipices, or
in Flats (mounted indoors, etc.)

Living with the enemy

whereas we have not made an accomodation
in the world as it is
and their lack of generosity
is enough, nearly, to take
the breath away from a crocodile

The metric system

The metric system is as full of shit
as the people who invented it†

too small in the small measures
too big in the big measures
and wrong enough in the middle
to push a new set of wrenches

What difference does it make
pure invention is just another idea.

---

† See John Michel on the atheism
and consequent unnaturalness
of The System.

next year will be the 100th
anniversary of 1877

37

Recycling is an after-work recreation.
Recreation, social conversation
incorporating cheap wine and an
Aluminum plan for tomorrow
by noon, or whenever the headache's gone.
Thin, flat rolled stock
fabricated cans are at the heart of it.

Recycling has grown to be
a major part of the pollution industry

39

Recreation
wrecks the nation

40

the family is
as big as the unit
shld have got

SF 27 Dec. '76 (V.R.)

Rancho Canaille, or Propositions for Living with
                the metaphor of Cancer

1. Annoying habits are always
cumulative in a closely packed (packaged) society

2. People who let the straw
roll over the coke are hideous

3. Nature is indispensable
but not necessary

Hall of Flowers

Yre so cheap minded
yr shoes squeak when you Talk

43

Suctorial

The qualities of an established necrosis:

A flourishing, abundant, moral conscientiousness
which is in the same time/instance, scarcely
manifested, and in fact can't be manifested because
it is essentially dishonest & self serving and
"used" to promote a "program", it is the rationale
of co-option parading as *cooperation*—"that's
progress," and "improvement":
                         collaboration w/Satan

gnawed tongues

they gnawed their
tongues for pain

Torture

"...because thou art lukewarm, and neither hot nor cold, I will spew thee out of my mouth."

Rev. 3:16

The Sonoma County Line: They always had a dirty sink

Obviously, anyone so literal minded
should not have gone to India & Pakistan
You brought back germs like other
people bring back hand-painted pots from mexico

Tortured

There are a lot of confused people around
And some of them think they should have a Homosexual experience

the sky is fixed
and we revolve
I never saw that
until recently
when I looked at the sky
all thru the livelong night

The Death of Howard Hughes

The story is not tragic because
his control is not to be seriously
questioned. The testimony of the aides,
or if one prefers, the "Mormon
Guard," is as the droppings of pink-eyed Rabbits.

Hughes

nobody, after 4 crashes is
gonna resist the
needle in the groin

Rediform: 30 gal. water from corp. yd.

The boys at the corporation yard
are looking smugger & smugger,
and I don't blame them at all.
It must be unusually hard
to deal water, yet there comes
that inevitable time when drought
makes even them bureaucrats.

Super

1. ceded
2. tanker
3. fluid (helium)
4. duper
5.

In defense of Quality

I'm no hater but I've heard
a considerable amount of soft incrimination
about that state lately
from types who profess to shrink from it.

It was Christmas Day,
so understand that protection
I decided to look hate up
and found it to be
what I guessed
before I walked over to the book.

I won't presume to
save you the trip, of course
we know better than that.

22 January

You know what I think?
I think La Jolla is heaven,
& PSA is limbo.

One of the increasingly urgent searches in writing
today is to find an adequate exclamation

The news tonight is mostly Hemoglobin
the Sunny Southland soggy with rain
What we have to have
is rainfall which comes down
faster than the ground will absorb it
so that it runs off into Lake Mendocino.
Yet such a rain would surely loosen
a lot of rocks which would come tumbling down.

Fortunately it looks as though
the West's leading powers think so too.

At this stage the difference derived from
their falling or not is marginal
and offers only a rather perverse case
in favor of stopping the rain. Yet
just as surely, expectations from the rain
overdue too long only breed the crass
and the people are aching to water the grass.
      3 Jan. 1977

The Evolution of Energy from Tennessee to Cumbria

It is generally pointless
to peddle the news in a poem†
unless, perhaps, one's practice
is in Costa Rica
and large scale events
are truly large
like Vesco enplaning

But an exception seems ordered
by the disclosure that β-in-air's
danger is signalled the sound of yodelling
down at the reactor site

---

† That the poem itself might or might not
be news is not what we're talking about.

Wanted

Some apprentice
should take on
the revival of E.E. Cummings
right about now.
We've had simple-mindedness
too long.

Manzanita

She is the richest red I know
you can pull dead manzanita apart
but careful of the limbs, they break
with great tension, explode in the word

Drier than bone, even in the rain
and usually standing, unlike oak
which falls all over the place.

I see a lot of people
reading on 101

60

Jimtown

The first assumption was somebody
named Jim lived there, perhaps
in a hut. But, tonight
chasing narcissus, drifting
into Narcotics, discovered
the 1890 common name
for Datura Stramonium to be
Jamestown weed

Whereas

Poetry is now mostly government product
the work of our non-existent critics
is unnecessary, the grades assigned
to meat will do nicely:
      Prime
      choice
      good
      commercial
      utility
      canners

Night Watchman, look to my flashlight

The common duty of the poet
in this era of massive dysfunction
& generalized onslaught upon alertness
is to maintain the plant
to the end that the mumbling horde
bestirs its prunéd tongue.

It is dangerous to be alive

Not all ventriloquists have dummies
Be wary of anyone who speaks through unmoving lips

101

numbers are the only entities
which don't lie

Time definitely
repeats itself.
That's it's only job.

66

those hunchbacks out back have a lot of crust
(tho no neck)

dancing in the morning sun
trying to cure their neurotic dog

Evolution[†]

The species managed its connection
in such a way

as to characterize the world
by characterization

[†] Really, no kidding, I'm not trying to make you think.

Grammatical problem†

The wages of promiscuity
is death.

---

† A take on the new clapp.

Eternal Vigilance (AM 101)

Sometimes coursing this
Parallel separated by zero
I'd rather be playing golf
And turn into a plain goof

The Word (20 January 1977)

Moved was a bit too classy
to be used to note an emotion
and I doubt that it occurred to him.
And who knows, it might
have seemed too Lowell-like
if it had crossed his mind

Sentimental, to be sure, cheap,
imported and ordinary

the script, but not necessarily the cure

for Northern California
is Southern California

72

Trailers

Cotati & Roehnert Park are the county slums
the segmentations of a Methadon tapeworm

People who call in are sick

"The main function of work
is to kill time."

                                        R. P. Warren

Admission of error is a weakness of judgement
if one senses beforehand that it will be seen
as a weakness

75

Post '76

Knowing how to speak English
in this country has become
about the biggest liability around.

76

Listen, if anybody out there's
saying, you know, there's
something new, and something
else or other's not, well,
they should look it up.

Useful

How to light a dead joint driving

78

Alaska is
the Raquel Welch
of landscape

79

The Plague: just another Metaphysical question

Are flies bred in dogshit
more domestic and dangerous than those
from other sources
for instance, those bred
from the shit of horses?

A Mild Threat

I'm going to put you in a petri dish
and there I'm going to grow you
not all of you, though, for instance
I'm not going to grow your head
and I'm not going to grow your body

The Whiner, Obnoxious as ever, at latest report

The child was even weirder
than the progenitors,
Loud, Spitting,
Rude and Offensive
with multiple and brittle defenses.
No wonder they caved into
his every devious whim.
They knew, because he was their offspring,
he was the test of their very worst aspects
and that non-compliance
would be a repudiation
of their very own worst selves
and so they supported a social menace
in order to hide their own, inner catastrophe.

Books I have read while Driving†

---

† The same rule applies here as in writing while driving, keep yr eye on the road.

101

The poet must always
be loyal to the poem
no matter what
other forms may beckon

The Rape of Deer Creek as it passed thru Lot ?
Section etc. Plat ? etc. by a hominid named Miller,
a former resident of mean local reputation

This is a case in which
the poem is summarized in the title.

In the Antiquity of habit,
we find the cave dweller
cast his bones in a certain corner
and that the giant ground sloth,
gone these past 11 thousand years,
encaved his yellow scat in Arizona.†

---

† And still burning. *Newsweek*, Vol. LXXXIX, No.8

Happiness is a violent emotion
which makes it easy to fake

86

I wouldn't go back for god's foot
if I'd dropped it on the road

87

Humanity divides neatly
into two categories
those who want to go
& those who want to stay

It is said poetry audiences
have one of the highest tedium tolerances
in the business, and that
this is proven by their willingness
to sit still for nearly anything.

However, I've always assumed
the opposite, and that, in fact
their steely determination
is one of the finest instruments
of modern times.

One must not be guilty
of lowering the ideal
by way of the false claims of kindness

It's an undeniable Law:
needle freaks shut their eyes
swallow their voices
& lie

At Jack Spicer's Bar

I never knew Jack Spicer
but that's not extraordinary (aire)
lots of people didn't. There
is a breeze thru here
pushed by soft rushing Italian
& "gimme a drink, I woke up nervous
this morning" is the common
Protestant salutation

Television & Children

The viewing cannot be censored
All T.V. content is alike
the uniformity is strict
the argument itself is not even
T.V.'s final joke: the whole thing's
violent,† from switch on to switch off.

Only the time can be cut, and that
might be the sole superiority
of English over American viewing,
there's less of it.

---
† Electron storm bombardment.

"one must not be unkind"
because it is demeaning
to the person, but not because
it is uninteresting practice

I don't give a dog turd
for stupidity
or averageness
or agreement
or mass culture
or straight talk
or who likes it
or who sells it
or who buys it

Manzanita (II)

I learned something about
Manzanita, how red it is
How hard and with what
a fine blue flame it burns
and finally that it is
"disturbed" and by extrapolation
that the use of it will be
disturbing

But the red eyed fuckers
next door didn't even learn
that
they burned propane the
whole damn time. The central
fact of wood was in their
wooden-legged stomping
across the 100,000 square
centimeters of ripped linoleum.

A protest against still another empty-minded choice

I've acquired this political problem
since I returned to North Beach

Every day now, for a while,
I've been handed a yellow piece of paper
which tells me to normalize
and just last week I saw
a banner spanning Grant Street
over in the China section
which told me to *not* normalize

I'm just a simple american†
which means that I don't *object*
to the normal, yet
the *not* normal of course interests me more.

---

† I.e., a fate-torn traveller.

Another tobacco poem

If all wastes were to be inhaled
the most important health hazard
would be the induction of lung cancer
                              Boulder, Colo. June 1977

The intellection of patterns

Heavy & subtle, like a regular
structure kept together w/honey

I have an excellent, if unconventional, memory

100

After-effects of WW II: Washington Square,
San Francisco 1977

"Hey boy,
Wha you do that for?"

There is a fight between the
Chinese and the Italians
and the Japanese side
with the Italians.

I can believe Panama is the most
beautiful isthmus in the world
on the sole evidence of her name

102

1 Billion Chinese are telling me
the gang of 4 are wrong?
Doesn't this seem out of proportion?

A reminder to the folks
back home, in La Jolla,
that all that can be known
has always been known
and that the reason
this simulation
has value is not parallel
to the conspiracy of Pontiac
but is parallel to the fact
that Geo. Washington was a land speculator

Success?

I never had to worry about success
Coming from where I come from
You were a success the minute you left town

The Burr Quote

Law is anything which is
Boldly asserted
and plausibly maintained.

The Dee Young Quote
(in Boulder)

"Religion is the last bastion of Free Enterprise"

now & then there is a chance
(I've rarely had the chance) to follow
the progress of my coordinates. There was
a report concerning Inuvik & Aklavik
                            from Vic D'or

a brief from Tom Clark on his flight
along the line connecting T.J. & El Paso†
(America)

---

† Flat & rough, like the inside of a casting

The song of the vulgar boatmen

You will sink into the spiritual darkness of the animal kingdom
And suffer infinite miseries of bondage, dumbness & torpor.

At least one increase has maintained itself
in the intermontane West:
dumb fucks in pickup trucks

The caucasian horde completes
a long and linear series of booty invasions
There is an attempt at times
to be both cutting and kind
thru the use of the word entrepreneurial
But let's leave it at Booty
which has a nastiness derived from the nursery

Alaska Revisited

I would have a lot more interest
in reincarnation if there were
less insistence on meat in the transmutations
But perhaps it is too ambitious
to dream of one's return as a glacier

Not so bad after all

The keynote speaker,
A Theologian from Somewhere
Explained that "one"
Could have pleasure
And God too.

A question of appetite

What was the salt water crocodile's favorite war? WW II.

Colorado

I've always felt that the Transient
Should have the promptest attention
Its necessities are strongest in the short run
And precisely because its condition is worse in the long run.

Whole Cars, full of dogs

The first thing that happens
When children go
Is dogs show up

Au Barre, in The Gold Hill Inn

Working in a university
is the lowest form of snobbery

a poem w/a french sound

Coca don't grow
in mexico

But quite a few
poppies do

(or poppy do)

I wish they could all be california cars[†]

"At the apogee, we get values;
at twilight, worn & defeated,
we abolish them. Fascination
of decadence—of the ages
when the trucks have no
further life... when they
pile up like skeletons in
the desiccated, pensive soul,
in the boneyard of dreams..."

[†] A realigning of Cioran.

"The Party"†

It always ends with a party

It is appalling that anyone
Should seek to be the agent of Shock
But only appalling as a proposition.
Farmed by action, it is amazing
or vulgar. Amazing is a rendering
Free from *everything*, and therefore
It is amazing. Vulgar, well, vulgar.††

It is the interdiction of meat
and therefore not light and
therefore not good for anybody.
We must resist this dictum
With our whole will,
Should it acquire the status of a real threat.

---
† By E.S. & Co.
†† "Those of you who wish to leave will not be given a refund," or, "You can check out any time you want, but you can never leave."
                          25 December 1977

2nd Chautauqua

It's retrograde to set up gods
But it's something to do

Take the 4 wheel drive,
for instance: It is the barbarians'
escape vehicle, their only instrument
against the shock   of truth

3rd Chautauqua

I can't figure out why *anybody'd*
be surprised that Journalists
serve the see aye A. They're
the perfect double agents. The press
pass alone is access enough,
but when you stir in all that
dripping sanctimony about the truth
you've pulled back the classic cover.
                                        Autumn, 1977

4th Chautauqua

It is easy to see in Boulder
what spreads the news of wealth
It is a rock of much size
and great weight emplaced on the lawn.

For the most part,
one feels friendly toward rocks
and wishes them well.

It seems equally clear, here,
that of mammalian life
it is the squirrel which will survive
the storm, not bicyclists
and certainly not skateboards.

5th Chautauqua

The organ of memory is destroyed
systematically in our children
or teased with the meanest statistics.

La Culpa

There is a certain sense
In which Ignorance is a pleasure
That is why it is so wide
Spread.

Advice revised

never use a return address†

---

† The snow doesn't.

The Bible

Before they ate the apple
They could talk?
Better ignore that flaw.

The Human Truck

Gimme a glass of gas
Said the jogger
as he trotted up the hill

(and in Dutch. . .

De Menselijke Truck

Geef me een glas benzine,
Zei de trimmer
Terwijl hij tegen de berg opzwoegde

Ed Dorn by Tom Clark

This
first edition
of Yellow Lola
formerly titled Japanese Neon
(Hello La Jolla, Book II) printed in
November 1980 by Mackintosh & Young
consists of a trade edition in wrappers; 161
numbered copies; & 26 lettered copies with a page
of holograph in the poet's hand. Numbered
and lettered copies have been signed by
the poet and handbound in boards
by Linda Benet. Design by
Graham Mackintosh and
set in Trump
Medieval.